Colorful World of Animals

Macaws

by Cecilia Pinto McCarthy

Consulting Editor: Gail Saunders-Smith, PhD

Consultant: Anne R. Hobbs
Public Information Specialist
Cornell Lab of Ornithology
Ithaca, New York

CAPSTONE PRESS
a capstone imprint

Pebble Plus is published by Capstone Press,
151 Good Counsel Drive, P.O. Box 669, Mankato, Minnesota 56002.
www.capstonepub.com

Books published by Capstone Press are manufactured with paper
containing at least 10 percent post-consumer waste.

Library of Congress Cataloging-in-Publication Data
McCarthy, Cecilia Pinto.
  Macaws / by Cecilia Pinto McCarthy.
    p. cm.—(Pebble plus. Colorful world of animals)
  Includes bibliographical references and index.
  Summary: "Simple text and full-color photos explain the habitat, range, life cycle, and behavior of macaws while
emphasizing their bright colors"—Provided by publisher.
  ISBN 978-1-4296-6049-5 (library binding)
  1. Macaws—Juvenile literature. I. Title.
  QL696.P7M37 2012
  598.7'1—dc22

2011000268

Editorial Credits
Katy Kudela, editor; Lori Bye, designer; Svetlana Zhurkin, media researcher; Laura Manthe, production specialist

Photo Credits
Alamy/Danita Delimont, 7
Dreamstime/Björn Höglund, 4–5, 8–9; Izaokas Sapiro, 20–21; Photosaurus, 11; Subhash Pathrakkada Balan, cover;
    Terry Evans, 15
Nature Picture Library/Jim Clare, 19
Photolibrary/Peter Arnold/SMuller, 12–13
Shutterstock/Carlos Moura, 16–17; Elenaphotos21, 1

Note to Parents and Teachers

The Colorful World of Animals series supports national science standards related to life science.
This book describes and illustrates macaws. The images support early readers in understanding
the text. The repetition of words and phrases helps early readers learn new words. This book
also introduces early readers to subject-specific vocabulary words, which are defined in the
Glossary section. Early readers may need assistance to read some words and to use the Table of
Contents, Glossary, Read More, Internet Sites, and Index sections of the book.

Printed in the United States of America in North Mankato, Minnesota.
032011
006110CGF11

Table of Contents

Rain Forest Birds

Bright feathers cover macaws from head to tail. These birds seem easy to spot. But high in the trees, their rainbow colors look like flowers or fruit.

Macaws are a kind of parrot.

They live in Mexico, Central

America, and South America.

Most macaws live in rain forests.

Some like drier areas.

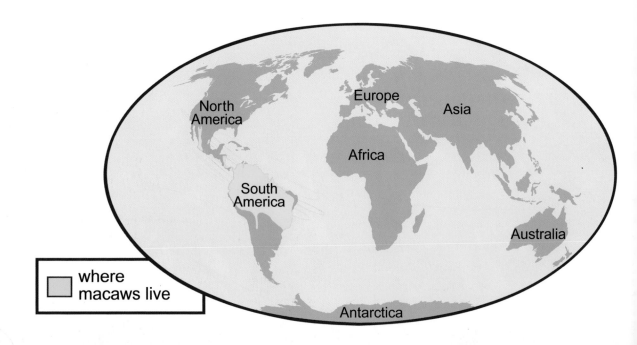

where macaws live

7

Macaw Bodies

There are 18 kinds of macaws. These birds have long tails and strong wings. Adults weigh between 4.5 ounces (128 grams) and 3.2 pounds (1.45 kilograms).

Macaws eat nuts, flowers, and fruit. They use their strong toes to grasp food. Crunch! Macaws' thick, curved beaks easily crack nutshells.

Staying Together

Macaws live in flocks

of up to 30 birds.

They roost and fly together.

Members watch for danger.

Harpy eagles hunt

young macaws.

Screech! Squawk!

Macaws make warning calls

when a predator is near.

Hatching and Growing

Macaws choose one mate for life. The female lays two to four eggs in a hole in a tree or cliff. The male feeds her while she warms the eggs.

Crack! The eggs hatch

23 to 30 days later.

Both parents feed the chicks.

In three to four months,

chicks are ready to fly.

chick

Like most parrots,

macaws can live long lives.

Scientists think some macaws

live up to 50 years in the wild.

Glossary

beak—the hard, pointed part of a bird's mouth

chick—a young bird

cliff—a high, steep wall of rock or earth

flock—a group of the same kind of animal; members of flocks live, travel, and eat together

harpy eagle—one of the world's largest and most powerful eagles; it is found in the rain forests of Central and South America

hatch—to break out of an egg

mate—the male or female partner of a pair of animals

predator—an animal that hunts other animals for food

rain forest—a thick forest where a great deal of rain falls

roost—to settle down for rest or sleep

Read More

Ganeri, Anita. *Macaw.* A Day in the Life: Rain Forest Animals. Chicago: Heinemann Library, 2011.

Rockwood, Leigh. *Parrots Are Smart!* Super Smart Animals. New York: PowerKids Press, 2010.

Internet Sites

FactHound offers a safe, fun way to find Internet sites related to this book. All of the sites on FactHound have been researched by our staff.

Here's all you do:

Visit *www.facthound.com*

Type in this code: 9781429660495

Super-cool stuff! Check out projects, games and lots more at www.capstonekids.com

Index

Word Count: 209

Grade: 1

Early-Intervention Level: 16